To Jaylee, Sophia, Sadie, and Mila, may your
light continue to shine bright always.

To my beautiful mother, wonderful father,
and amazing husband, thank you for always
reminding me of my own beautiful light.

To all of my students who have graced my path
and for the children whose hands hold this
book, may you make our world a better place
by remembering your beautiful light.

www.mascotbooks.com

Pet'a Shows Misun the Light

Eighth printing. This Mascot Books edition printed in 2021.

For more information, please contact:
Mascot Books
620 Herndon Parkway, Suite 320
Herndon, VA 20170
info@mascotbooks.com

Library of Congress Control Number: 2017912928

CPSIA Code: PRT0521H
ISBN-13: 978-1-68401-492-7

Printed in the United States

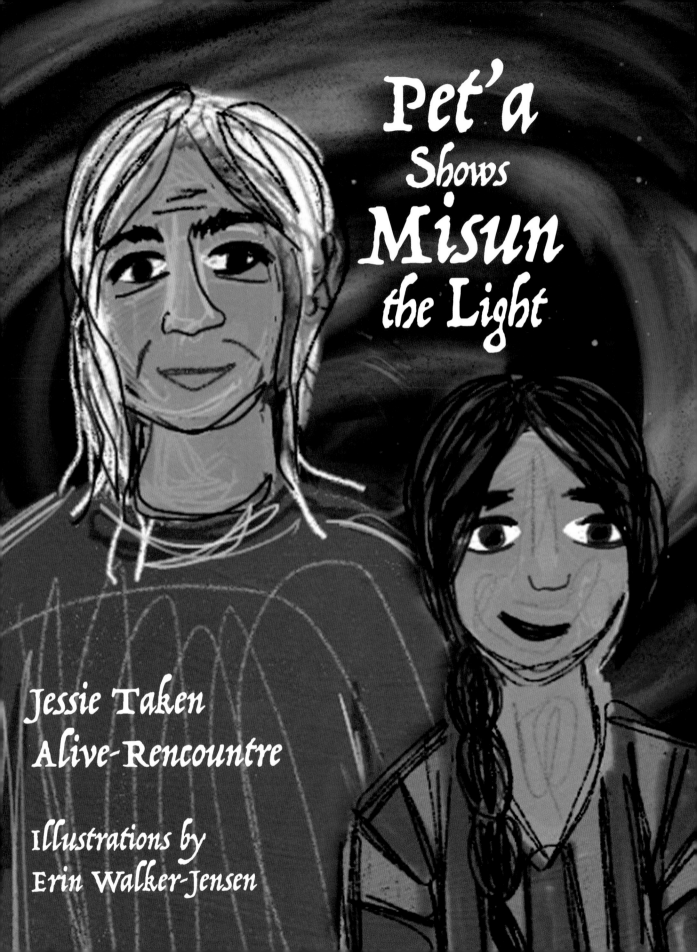

Pet'a
Shows
Misun
the Light

Jessie Taken
Alive-Rencountre

Illustrations by
Erin Walker-Jensen

It was a cool August night and Misun's grandmother hollered up the stairs that it was time for bed. Like every night, Misun put his books away and went downstairs to give his grandparents a hug good night.

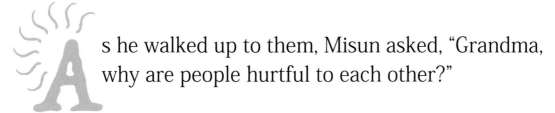s he walked up to them, Misun asked, "Grandma, why are people hurtful to each other?"

"What do you mean, Misun?" Grandmother asked.

"Well, there's a girl in my class named Lucy. Everyone makes fun of her old clothes and dirty shoes. During recess they leave her out of games, and sometimes they even hit her. Why do they do that?"

Grandmother quietly asked, "You're not mean to her, are you?"

"No!" Misun said. "It just makes me feel bad, and I don't understand why people treat others that way."

Grandmother put her sewing down on her lap and said, "I'm glad that you're not one of those kids. But you also have to help those who are hurting. If you see someone being hurt and you don't help them, you're almost just as wrong as those bullies. When you see those kids hurting Lucy, you need to be brave and either tell them to stop or get help from a teacher."

"I will, but I still don't understand why some people are so mean in the first place."

"Sometimes we don't know the answers to everything," Misun's grandfather said. "Our universe is filled with questions. My grandfather always told me to go outside, look up in the sky, and ask for understanding. The answer will be given to you."

onfused, Misun said good night and went back upstairs. In his bedroom, he looked out his window at the moon and stars that were shining bright. A cool breeze made his curtains dance peacefully.

Misun thought about Lucy. He also thought about his best friend Thomas, whose dad was always so mean, and his friend Sammy, whose mom was always drinking and doing drugs. He thought about the news he heard earlier about war and people fighting each other. And lastly, he thought about his mother, who left him with his grandparents when he was two years old and never came back.

With so many questions in his mind, Misun remembered what his grandfather had said. He looked out at the big, beautiful night sky and asked for understanding about people's behavior before he went to sleep.

A knock on his window woke him. Outside his window, there was a beautiful blue ball of light that made him feel safe, calm, and loved. As he pushed his curtain aside, the blue light floated in. Misun rubbed his eyes, and when he lowered his hands, he saw an old man standing where the blue light had been.

"Who are you?" Misun asked.

The old man smiled. "My name is Pet'a. I would like to show you something that will help you understand. Will you come with me?"

Misun nodded. Pet'a gently took Misun's hand and they floated out the window. They flew up through the gorgeous white clouds and the moonlight until they were far above the Earth.

 "**M**isun, look down at Grandmother Earth closely," Pet'a said. "What do you see?"

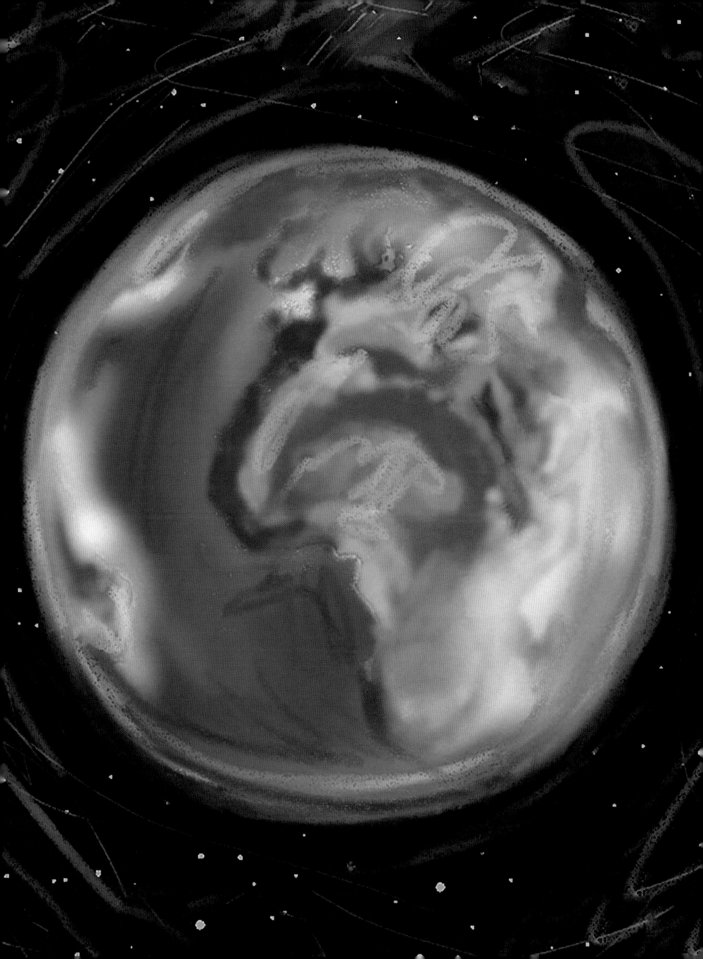

Misun looked and saw people standing with bright beautiful lights in them, while others crouched to the ground. "I see some people with lights and some people who don't have any lights."

Pet'a smiled. "Are you sure? Look closer."

Misun looked closer at the people who were kneeling and realized that they did have lights! They were just very dim and hard to see.

"Why do you think some have brighter lights and others are dimmer?" Pet'a asked.

Misun saw that those with dim lights were like Lucy, the kids who hurt Lucy, Thomas's dad, Sammy's mom, and his own mom. That's when everything made sense! "Those with the dim lights forgot that they have lights," Misun said. "They are sad, angry, lost, sick, and scared."

"You are right, grandson," Pet'a said. "We are all born into the world with lights so bright that people are drawn to us. Over the years, others hurt us with their words and actions and we begin to forget how beautiful we are."

It was like he had been given new eyes. Misun saw how so many people on Earth were hurting and how they acted out of their hurt. His eyes swelled with tears.

"Grandson, look at those with the bright lights," Pet'a said, pointing. "They have experienced a lot of hurt, too, but they have made a choice to remember how special they are. They have made a choice to treat others with kindness and love. They chose to have compassion and to forgive. They chose happiness. They remember where we come from. You see grandson, we all come from the same place. We all are born with a bright light. Those with the dim lights are not bad people. There are no bad people, only people with a lot of hurt."

As Misun looked, a person with a bright light went over to one with a dimmed light. "Watch closely," Pet'a said. The person with the bright light pulled up the one with the dimmed light, and as they stood, their dimmed light began to shine just as bright as the person who had helped them.

Before Misun knew it, the world began to shine as people treated each other with kindness and love. "They're all helping each other!"

"One person cannot change the world by themselves," Pet'a said. "But if we all work together and treat those around us with kindness and love, it spreads like fire. Sometimes all it takes is a simple smile."

All the world was lit now and the feeling that radiated from Grandmother Earth was a long-forgotten feeling that Misun couldn't quite place.

"When we are born, all we know how to do is love. We don't know anything else. The acts of hate and selfishness are learned from others. If we can all remember that feeling of love and remember how important each of us are, our world would be so beautiful."

et'a's eyes started to swell with tears. "Why do you cry?" Misun asked.

Pet'a pointed to his right eye and said, "I have tears coming from this side because I see how many people are hurting and lost. Too many children cry every day and start to forget how special they are."

Pet'a wiped his tear and pointed to the other side. "On this side, I cry tears of joy, for now you and other children understand how simple it is to change the world to one full of kindness and love. They are tears of hope because I know that many children like you will understand and remember. Children like you will solve your problems not through fighting, but rather with your brilliant minds. I know that you will have compassion for one another and help each other. I know that children like you will remember how special and sacred they are."

Pet'a smiled and wiped the tears from his eyes. "Come now grandson, it's time to go home."

et'a and Misun started back down to Grandmother Earth. As they got closer, Misun felt like a mask had been removed from his eyes. He understood why the world was the way it was and what he had to do to make it a better place.

Before Misun knew it, he was back in his room. Pet'a said, "Grandson, never forget what you have learned tonight. Help others find their light. But also know that allowing your own light to shine bright will remind others of their own light, and let their light shine bright as well."

"I will," Misun said. He turned to give Pet'a a hug, but Pet'a was gone. Instead, there was a beautiful blue light floating into the night sky. Misun watched it fly higher and higher until it took its place amongst the stars.

Misun thought about what his grandparents had told him earlier and understood what they wanted him to learn. He smiled, closed his eyes, and went to sleep, excited to do what he needed to do to make the world a better place.

About the Author

Jessie is a Hunkpapa Lakota from the Standing Rock Sioux Reservation. She makes her home in the beautiful Black Hills with her husband and their four beautiful daughters. Jessie has worked as a school counselor in the elementary and high school setting, where she has crossed paths with many beautiful children who have shared their stories of hurt over the years. She has been inspired to help children overcome their hurts through forgiveness, compassion, and understanding.

About the Illustrator

Erin Walker-Jensen is an artist from Fort Yates, ND. She grew up on a farm on the Standing Rock Reservation. Erin has been creating artwork since she was a young child. She resides in Mandan, ND with her husband and children.